BLAST OFF!

Written by
KIRSTIE WATSON

Illustrated by
NINA KHALOVA

For my mum (AKA Grandma), thanks for being
the best mum in the whole universe!

Kirstie x

Telltale Tots Ltd.
www.telltaletots.co.uk

First published in the United Kingdom by Telltale Tots Publishing 2022

ISBN: 978-1-914937-09-5

A CIP catalogue record for this book is available from the British Library.
Text and illustrations copyright © Kirstie Watson 2022

BLAST OFF!

Jack and Grace were very excited. Grandma was putting them to bed tonight, and bedtimes with Grandma were the BEST.

"Grandmaaaa," said Grace, "can we play ONE more game before bed? Pleeeease."

"Okay," said Grandma, "I think there's time for one more little adventure. Where shall we go this time?"

"Yay! Let's go to the Moon!" said Jack, grabbing some cookies for the trip.

"Ready for countdown!" said Grace, excitedly.

"FIVE, FOUR, THREE, TWO, ONE, BLAST OFF!"

They all loved playing space explorers.

Together they'd picnicked on faraway moons...

...toured the Milky Way...

...and visited weird and wonderful planets.

"We'll have to zoom there quickly so we're back before Mum comes to tuck you in!" Grandma said, pushing their little ship to top speed.

WHOOOOSH!

"I wonder if we'll find any aliens on the Moon tonight!"
Grace wondered as Grandma dodged a meteorite.

"I hope so! I'd LOVE to meet an alien." Jack said hopefully.

Just then, they noticed a bright, twinkly light behind them.
At first, it looked like a star, but then It grew bigger and brighter.

"What on Earth is that?" asked Grace, rubbing her eyes.

"Whatever it is, it looks like it's following us!" said Jack.

Grandma pushed their spaceship as fast as it would go.
It was a race to the Moon that she was determined to win.

Their spaceship landed first; then the strange
light landed beside them with a bright **FLASH!**

They were surprised to see that it was actually...

...an alien spaceship.

Feeling a little afraid, they watched as the spaceship's
door opened and out stepped...

...a little green alien.

Jack and Grace couldn't believe their luck; they were finally meeting a real alien. "Hello!" they called.

The alien looked startled but happy to see them and replied with something they couldn't understand.

They had fun exploring the Moon together...

...sliding down craters...

...playing space tag...

...and Moon hide and seek.

Jack got out the cookies when they were tired of playing,
but the alien didn't seem very keen.

In return, the alien offered them a piece of a glowing green cake that smelled of jam and rotten eggs. To which they all politely said,

"NO, THANK YOU!".

All too soon, it was time to go home.

They said their goodbyes, promising to meet again soon.

Then Jack, Grace and Grandma jumped back into their spaceship.

But this time, nothing happened. The spaceship didn't move, and worst of all, it didn't WHOOOSH.

"Oh dear!" said Grandma. "I think we're out of fuel."

"Oh nooo! We're going to be stuck here forever!" Grace cried.

The alien didn't seem to understand at all. He just smiled and offered them some more green cake.

"No, thank you," said Grace, "we just want to go home. Mum will be coming to tuck us in soon, and if we're not back, she'll be worried."

Their spaceship rumbled as it suddenly burst into life.

"Thank you, THANK YOU!" said Jack. "It worked, and you've saved us!"

They waved goodbye as Jack began the launch sequence...

"FIVE, FOUR, THREE, TWO, ONE, BLAST OFF!"

A little while later, they landed back in their bedroom.

"Wow, Grandma, that was a brilliant space adventure!" Grace yawned.

"And I can't believe we finally met a real alien!" Jack said sleepily.

Grandma was just tucking them into bed as Mum popped
her head around the door to say goodnight.

"Phew, just in time," whispered Grandma.
"Goodnight, my little space explorers."

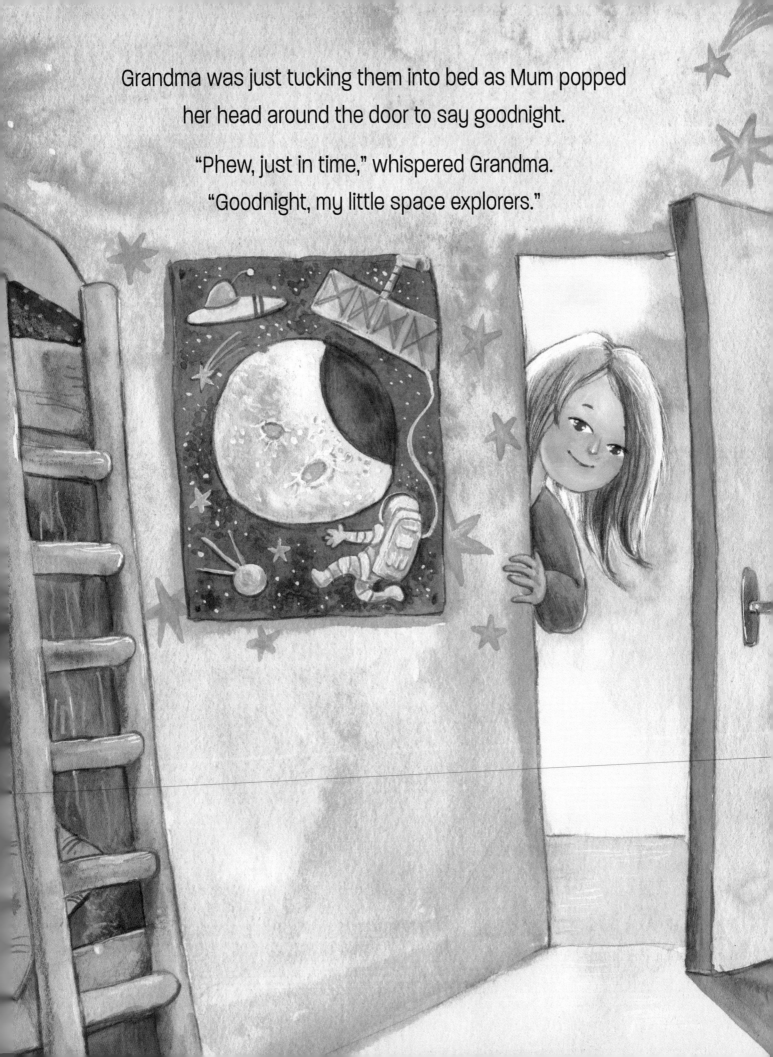

Jack and Grace snuggled into their beds and were asleep in...
Five, four, three, two, one...

ZZZZZZZZ!

THANK YOU FOR BUYING THIS BOOK!

I hope you've enjoyed this adventure with Grandma!

Did you know that reader reviews are even better than stinky green cake

for an author like me? They help bring attention to the book, and help others

decide if they'd like to buy it too. So, if you enjoyed this book, please consider...

1. Telling your **FRIENDS.**

2. Telling **ME!** Nothing makes my day like a message from a happy reader!

You can send me a message via: kirstiewatsonauthor.co.uk

3. Leaving an honest **REVIEW** on Amazon or Goodreads.

Kirstie x

GET YOUR FREE COLOURING PAGES!

Download from: kirstiewatsonauthor.co.uk/resources

FIND OUT MORE ABOUT KIRSTIE AND HER BOOKS:

f facebook.com/kirstiewatsonauthor

instagram.com/kirstie_watson_author

Printed in Great Britain
by Amazon

85169209R00022